This year, Chinese New Year begins on February 9.

Can you find these hidden objects?

pretzel

snake

palette

frog

candle

ice-cream cone

fish

star

ghost

bird

elephant

mitten

baseball

crescent moon

pencil

owl

carrot

Illustrated by Susan T. Hall

Highlights®

1

Fairy-Tale Favorites

Hans Christian Andersen, creator of *The Red Shoes* and other tales, was born on April 12, 1805 — 200 years ago.

flyswatter

needle

artist's brush

pencil

slice of pie

high-heeled shoe

THE UGLY DUCKLING

THE RED SHOES

THE RED SHOES

The Shadow

Can you find these hidden objects?

pear

lollipop

pennant

cane

mushroom

baseball cap

sea gull

sailboat

barbell

hairbrush

golf club

2

screwdriver

candle

banana

crayon

spoon

bell

tack

hockey stick

crescent moon

fishhook

cherries

balloon

ring

pickax

fishing pole

insect

musical note

straight pin

Illustrated by Lynn Adams

Highlights®

Pretty Parakeets

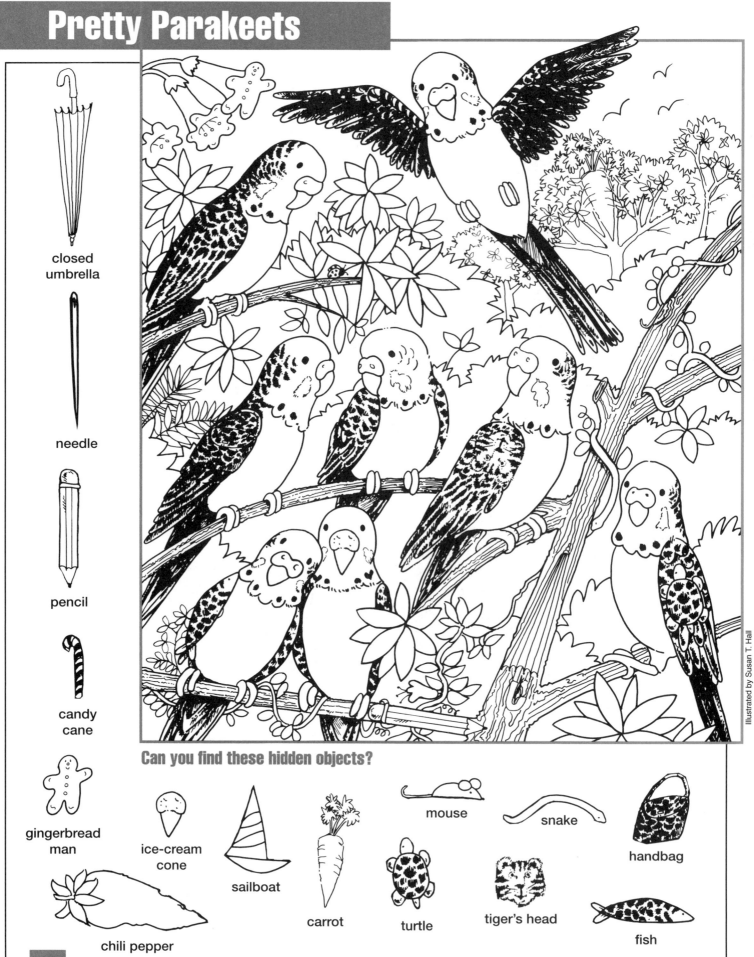

Can you find these hidden objects?

closed umbrella

needle

pencil

candy cane

gingerbread man

ice-cream cone

sailboat

carrot

mouse

snake

handbag

chili pepper

turtle

tiger's head

fish

Illustrated by Susan T. Hall

Highlights®

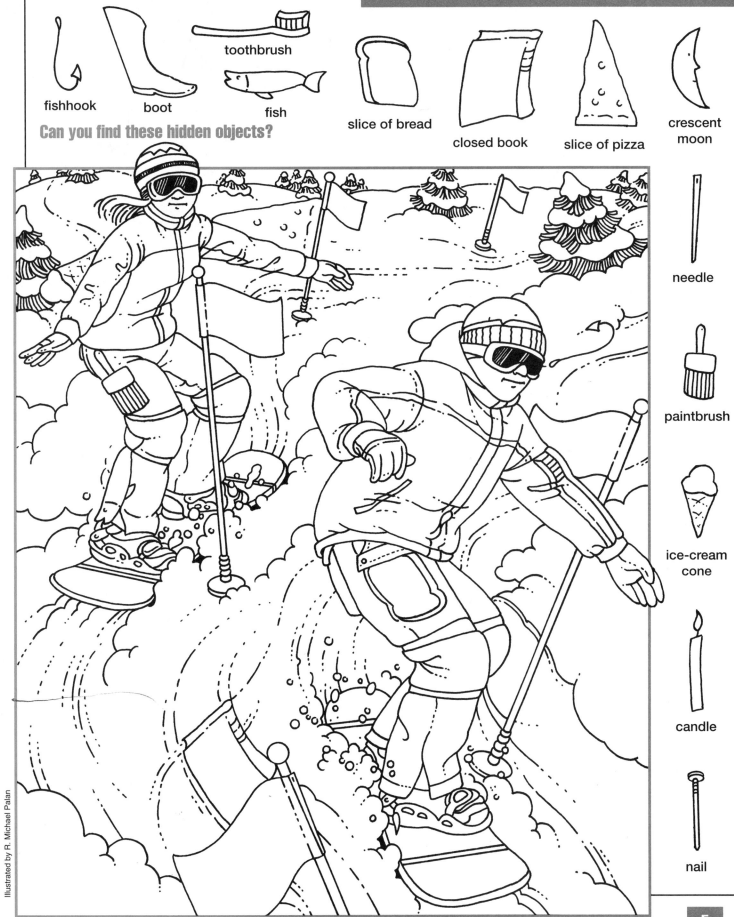

fishhook

boot

toothbrush

fish

Can you find these hidden objects?

slice of bread

closed book

slice of pizza

crescent moon

needle

paintbrush

ice-cream cone

candle

nail

Illustrated by R. Michael Palan

Highlights®

Running for a Touchdown

artist's brush

snail

comb

wishbone

open umbrella

Illustrated by Leslie Franz

Can you find these hidden objects?

slice of pie

ladle

mallet

snake

cat

horse

saltshaker

bird

carrot

chicken

mouse

Halloween is on a Monday this year.

shoe

baseball bat

screwdriver

ice-cream cone

sheep

slice of pie

exclamation point

number 4

bird

hat

pennant

Can you find these hidden objects?

letter B

letter E

closed book

lamp

needle

ladder

lollipop

Illustrated by Lynn Adams

Yard-Sale Bargains

nail

screwdriver

mallet

pencil

Can you find these hidden objects?

pennant

carrot

shovel

crown

sock

magnifying glass

toothbrush

ice-cream bar

Illustrated by Charles Jordan

Highlights®

ice-cream cone

adhesive bandage

banana

closed book

toothbrush

snake

fishhook

fork

house

eyeglasses

feather

nail

artist's brush

flag

pencil

comb

candle

needle

Can you find these hidden objects?

Illustrated by Sally Springer

Highlights®

basketball

spoon

kite

horseshoe

snail

LETTUCE

CARROTS

Can you find these hidden objects?

crescent moon

ring

star

teacup

heart

wishbone

bowl

crown

Illustrated by Diana Zourelias

Highlights®

Sandra Day O'Connor, the first woman appointed to the U.S. Supreme Court, celebrates her 75th birthday this year.

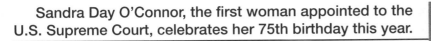

paper clip

caterpillar

slice of pizza

bird

pencil

heart

spoon

crown

toothbrush

candle

Can you find these hidden objects?

EQUAL JUSTICE UNDER LAW

SANDRA DAY O'CONNOR

SUPREME COURT OF THE UNITED STATES · SEAL OF THE ·

carrot

needle

artist's brush

Illustrated by Timothy Davis

Highlights®

nail

duck

fishhook

candle

golf club

Can you find these hidden objects?

toothbrush

teacup

musical note

crescent moon

wishbone

comb

pie

Highlights®

mushroom

spoon

hammer

saucepan

sailboat

candle

duck

open book

spool of
thread

ring

Can you find these hidden objects?

dog's head

muffin

pennant

mitten

bowl

Backyard Court

May is National Physical Fitness and Sports Month.

Illustrated by Sally Springer

pencil

tack

heart

hat

artist's brush

paintbrush

flag

golf club

drinking straw

Can you find these hidden objects?

wedge of cheese

thimble

nail

teacup

candle

jar

clothespin

needle

spoon

carrot

mug

crescent moon

14

Highlights®

Hungry Sparrows

slice of pie

kite

pushpin

safety pin

cupcake

bell

ice-cream cone

slice of cake

golf club

closed umbrella

candle

magic wand

Can you find these hidden objects?

Illustrated by Charles Jordan

Highlights®

September 18–24 is National Dog Week.

bowling pin

glove

paper clip

sailboat

pencil

SIGN IN PLEASE

DR. KENDALL VETERI

Can you find these hidden objects?

feather

slice of pie

fish

paintbrush

toothbrush

high-heeled shoe

heart

bat

bell

Illustrated by Timothy Davis

Highlights®

bell

crown

caterpillar

lamp

slice of lemon

cardinal

magnet

Can you find these hidden objects?

crescent moon

bowling ball

slice of pizza

needle

egg

heart

COTTON CANDY

ONE

Illustrated by Diana Zourelias

Highlights®

The Princess and the Pea

spool of thread

dog bone

mug

saltshaker

mitten

paintbrush

bottle

Illustrated by Maggie Swanson

Can you find these hidden objects?

open book

hairbrush

slice of cake

mushroom

slice of pie

baseball bat

fish

Highlights®

The Queen and Her Hive

bell

heart

sailboat

fish

coat hanger

horn

sock

open book

kite

Can you find these hidden objects?

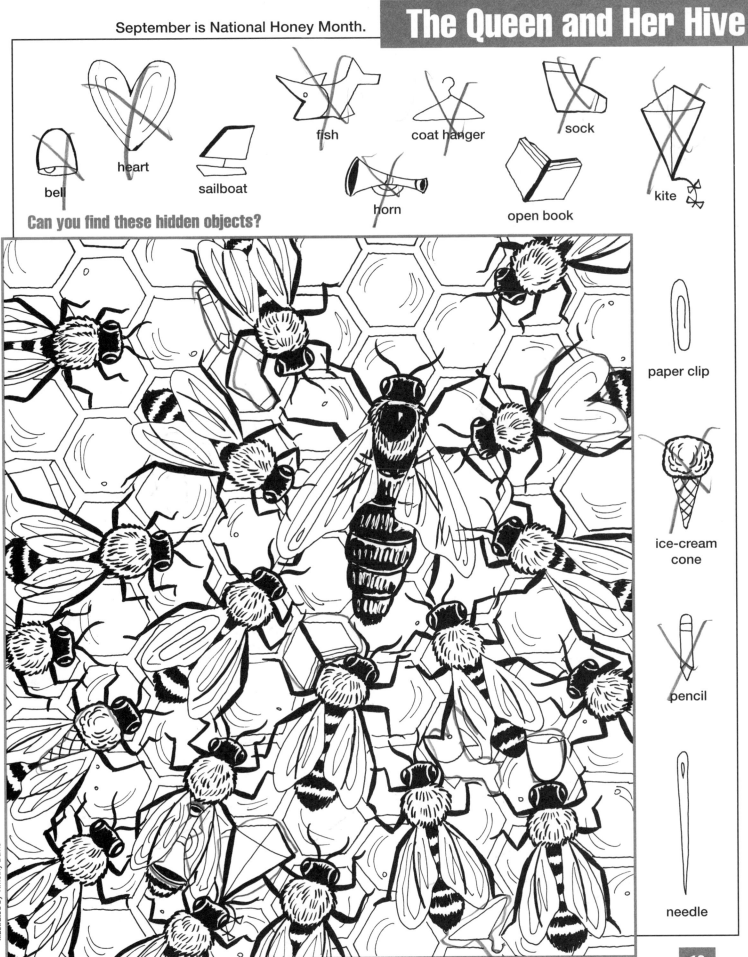

paper clip

ice-cream cone

pencil

needle

Illustrated by Timothy Davis

Highlights®

19

Animal Amusement Park

pennant

artist's brush

pushpin

pencil

Can you find these hidden objects?

slice of cake

flashlight

cupcake

bell

feather

crown

oilcan

slice of pizza

ice-cream cone

candle

golf club

slice of pie

ring

mallet

crayon

teacup

radish

spatula

mitten

nail

Illustrated by Charles Jordan

Historic Landing

Sailing from England, the Pilgrims arrived at what is now Plymouth, Massachusetts, in 1620—385 years ago.

pencil

crescent moon

toothbrush

sock

muffin

nail

Can you find these hidden objects?

slice of cake

bird

mushroom

snake

flowerpot

scissors

heart

thimble

needle

teacup

Illustrated by Sally Springer

Can you find these hidden objects?

banana
spoon
comb
fish
crown
needle
snake
bird
shoe
sailboat
kite
artist's brush
boot

Illustrated by Timothy Davis

Highlights®

23

Spring begins on March 20.

pennant

bottle

candle

mushroom

crown

crescent moon

Can you find these hidden objects?

ladle

key

high-heeled shoe

trowel

saw

sailboat

teacup

fish

toothbrush

Illustrated by Maggie Swanson

Highlights ®

artist's brush

snake

toothbrush

tube of paint

fork

spoon

wishbone

slice of pie

fishhook

heart

screwdriver

ice-cream cone

hammer

Can you find these hidden objects?

Illustrated by R. Michael Palan

Highlights®

A Visit to Saturn

Illustrated by Timothy Davis

needle

pencil

pear

ladle

Can you find these hidden objects?

boomerang

closed book

paper clip

ice-cream cone

paintbrush

slice of pie

comb

shoe

Highlights®

Can you find these hidden objects?

camera
ruler
worm
toothbrush
2 snakes
crown
cracker
pitcher
doughnut
flashlight
mallet
comb

slice of pizza
muffin
hammer
ring
slice of swiss cheese
squirrel
flowerpot

Illustrated by Larry Daste

Highlights®

27

Can you find these hidden objects?

slice of bread

sock

rabbit

pear

wishbone

slice of pizza

skunk

saltshaker

baseball cap

ruler

tea bag

bat

A Bike for Two

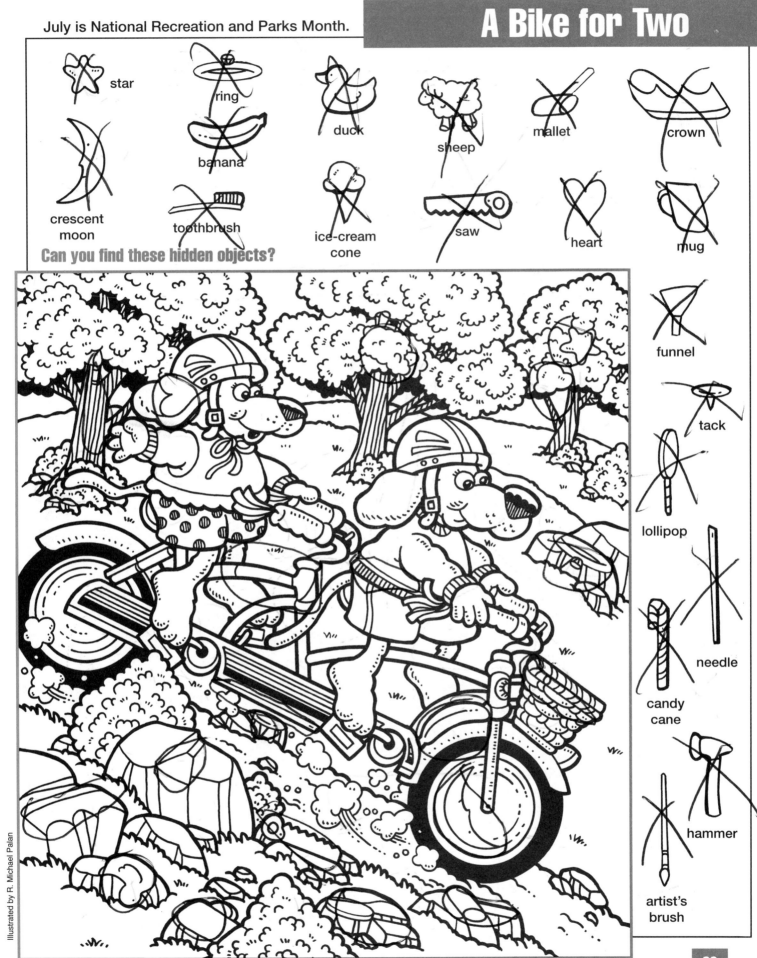

star

ring

duck

sheep

mallet

crown

crescent moon

banana

toothbrush

ice-cream cone

saw

heart

mug

Can you find these hidden objects?

funnel

tack

lollipop

needle

candy cane

hammer

artist's brush

Highlights®

May 23 is World Turtle Day.

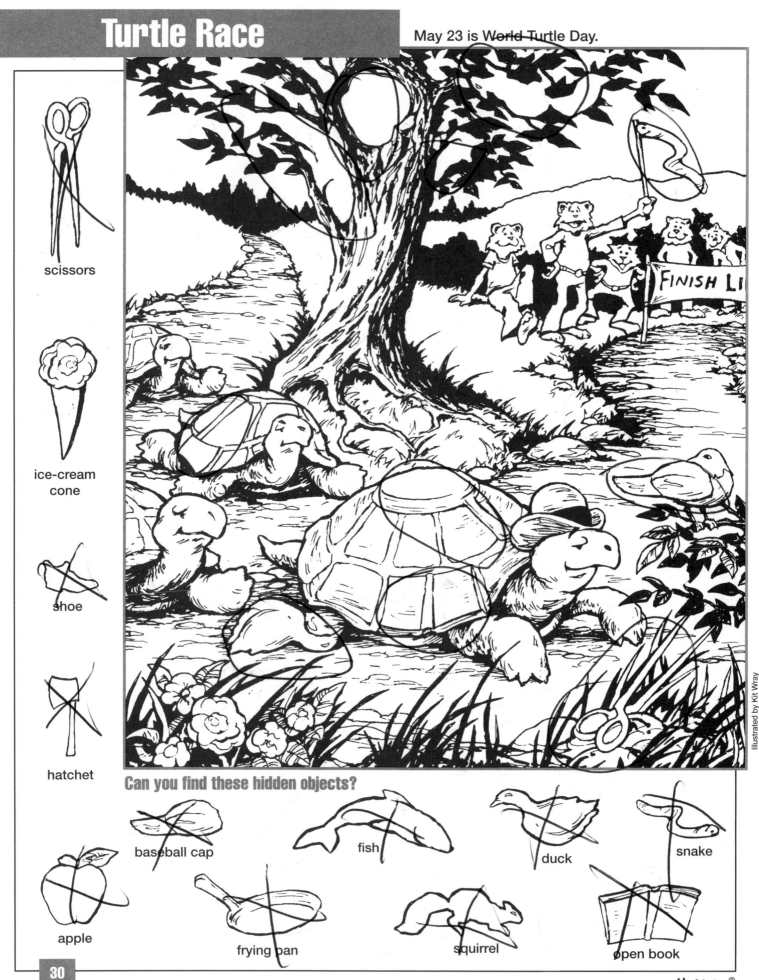

scissors

ice-cream cone

shoe

hatchet

Illustrated by Kit Wray

Can you find these hidden objects?

baseball cap

fish

duck

snake

apple

frying pan

squirrel

open book

mug

ring

paintbrush

saw

canoe

snail

mushroom

pear

button

tack

rabbit

toothbrush

whale

Can you find these hidden objects?

crescent moon

needle

heart

pennant

funnel

lollipop

boot

Illustrated by Linda Weller

Highlights®

Balloon Ride

The first nonstop crossing of North America in a hot-air balloon took place in 1980—25 years ago.

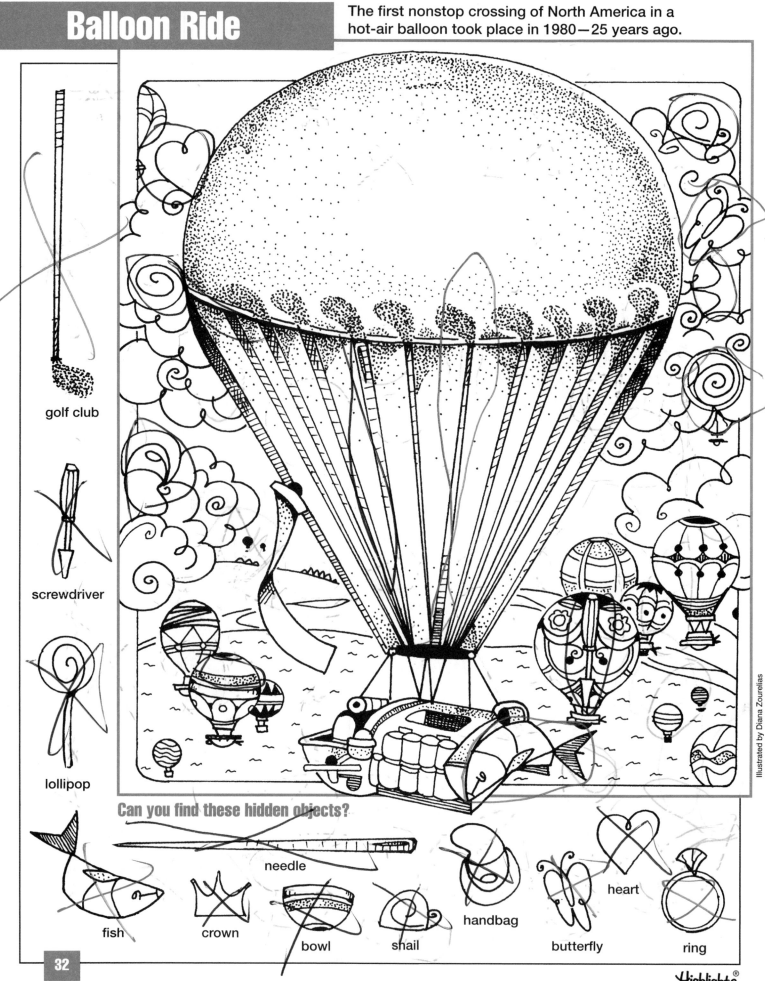

golf club

screwdriver

lollipop

Illustrated by Diana Zourelias

Can you find these hidden objects?

needle

fish

crown

bowl

snail

handbag

butterfly

heart

ring

September is National Chicken Month.

Will Cross for Corn

Can you find these hidden objects?

glove

banana

heart

megaphone

toothbrush

fish

slice of pie

tack

eyeglasses

sailboat

bell

paper clip

pencil

needle

Illustrated by Timothy Davis

Highlights®

November 13–19 is American Education Week.

ball

scrub brush

jar

mitten

screwdriver

Can you find these hidden objects?

mushroom

sock

paper airplane

mouse

lollipop

bowl

jump rope

Illustrated by George Wildman

Clown Class

butterfly

button

bowl

caterpillar

spoon

sock

paintbrush

slice of pie

Can you find these hidden objects?

wristwatch

hatchet

teacup

ice-cream cone

tack

Illustrated by David Helton

Highlights®

September is Square Dance Month.

candle

spatula

pencil

needle

Can you find these hidden objects?

hairbrush

closed book

radish

ballpoint pen

pushpin

hammer

bell

banana

mitten

slice of cake

artist's brush

golf club

screwdriver

hoe

mallet

paper clip

nail

ladle

light bulb

slice of pie

Illustrated by Charles Jordan

screwdriver

nail

pencil

carrot

Can you find these hidden objects?

fried egg

bird

jar

football

paper airplane

funnel

cupcake

button

Illustrated by George Wildman

Highlights®

Answers

▼Page 1

▼Pages 2–3

Highlights®

Answers

▼Page 4

▼Page 5

▼Page 6

▼Page 7

Highlights®

▼Page 8

▼Page 9

▼Page 10

▼Page 11

Answers

▼Page 12

▼Page 13

▼Page 14

▼Page 15

Highlights®

▼Page 16

▼Page 17

▼Page 18

▼Page 19

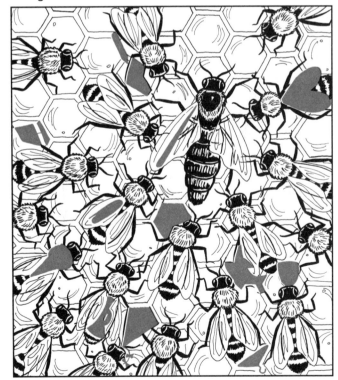

Answers

▼ Pages 20–21

▼ Page 22

▼ Page 23

Highlights®

▼Page 24

▼Page 25

▼Page 26

▼Page 27

Answers

▼Page 28

▼Page 29

▼Page 30

▼Page 31

▼Page 32

▼Page 33

▼Page 34

▼Page 35

Answers

▼Pages 36–37

▼Page 38

▼Cover